D1279643

LITTLE LAMB SHENANIGANS

by Ed Pacheco

Illustrations by Kristina Z. Young

Fuzzybear Press
Dartmouth, MA

User Discretion is Advised

WARNING!

THIS BOOK IS NOT
FOR SERIOUS
BEDTIME

This book is for GIGGLES and
SHENANIGANS before Bedtime

Every child has a special bedtime routine. Some children take a shower or a bath before bedtime, and some floss and brush their teeth.

Some may spend some quiet time listening to music or saying their prayers. Others just race right to bed after they have been told 10 times that it is past their bedtime!

Many children love to hear a
bedtime story before they are
tucked in.

This is a story about a little girl name Jenna Marie. During the day, Jenna is your usual little girl. She gets up in the morning, eats breakfast, gets dressed and even makes her own lunch, before leaving for school.

That's pretty impressive for only being 9 years old!

When she goes to school, she is an incredibly smart little girl. She loves to read and write and sing. She is a whiz at math and science, and during gym class she is one of the fastest runners in her whole school.

Kindness is very important to Jenna too. She tries to be a very kind girl every day. When she sees new people at school she goes out of her way to help the new children find their way around the school and makes sure no one sits alone at lunch or at the playground.

After school, when she gets home, she does her homework without being told (most of the time).

After dinner, she helps clear the dishes, feeds her pet cat Tyler and takes out the trash. Jenna really is an awesome little girl.

There only seems to be one thing that Jenna has trouble with, BEDTIME. Every night, Jenna has trouble getting to bed on time. If she is reading, she gets too distracted and forgets about getting ready. If she is listening to music, she gets distracted. If she is playing with her cat, Tyler, she forgets about getting ready. There is always something distracting Jenna from bedtime.

Sometimes at night, her grandma will call upstairs to her: "Jenna Dear, time to get ready for bed."

Jenna would respond, "Okay Grandma", but then quickly forget about bedtime and go back to reading.

A little while later, her grandpa, will call to her, "Little Jenna, time for bed." Jenna would call back, "getting ready, Grandpa", but then get distracted and go back to reading.

This would go on and on. Sometimes her Big Sister would call to her," Jenna, are you in bed yet?," to which she would say "Almost ready", and her other Sister would say, "Hey get ready for bed short stuff ," and Jenna would say, "I'm mostly in bed," even though she wasn't.

It was a terrible time, EVERY. NIGHT.

After everyone else would call her, Mom would come down the hall to her room and say "Jenna Marie!, It is time for bed" in a stern voice. Sadly her head would nod in agreement, but her feet would not move.

Unfortunately, it wasn't until her dad would say, in a big bear like voice, Jenna Marie, Time! For! BED!! When she heard this, she would quickly mark her page, and shuffle over to the bathroom to floss and brush her teeth, before someone came up stairs to tuck her in.

Usually, it was her dad who tucked her in at night. He would fluff her pillow and she would jump on the bed, burying her face into it.

Then she would flip over on her side, just as the blankets would fall on her with a big gush of wind before it.

One night, her dad asked her, "Why does it take so long for you to get to bed every night honey?" Jenna thought for a moment and finally answered, "I feel like I have a lot of energy left in my "battery" at night."

"Really?" Dad said with a deep, thoughtful look. After a moment of thinking, he said to her, "You know, when I was little, I used to have the same issue."

Jenna was shocked! "Really?" She asked.

"Yes, I would have so much energy at night that I would bounce on my bed for almost an hour, until my Nana would come in and sing me a song. It was a special song and by the end of it, I would be so tired, I wouldn't remember falling asleep. Even better was, I wouldn't get into trouble for having to be told so many times to get ready for bed!"

Jenna's eyes grew wide with excitement and she begged her dad, "Please! Please! Please! Sing me the song." He said he would, but he warned her, she would be *verrrrry* tired when it was over. She said that was okay, she was looking forward to it.

After he tucked her in, He sat on the foot of her bed
and in a smooth deep voice slowly started to sing:

"*I'm just a little lamb, look at me.*"

Now at first, Jenna did not think this song was very
special at all, but then it went on.

"I'm just a little lamb, cute as can be,"
She thought to herself as she closed her eyes, "Well yes I am very cute, but I still don't feel sleepy," but it continued:

"*I'm just a little lamb, my daddy loves me,*" She thought to herself, "Oh well that part is super sweet to hear, but I'm still not tired" …. And then, just when she thought it was over, she saw his hands slowly start moving and just as he sang the last line,

"I'm just a little lamb, He TICKLES me,"
He began tickling her feet!
She giggled and snorted and laughed so much that tears ran down her cheeks. He knew her feet were very Ticklish!

It was such a commotion, that her mom and sisters and grandpa and grandma all came running up to her room to see what the ruckus was about. When they got there, Jenna was red faced and laughing so hard that she still had tears coming down her face and her dad was tickling her feet so fast, he looked as if he was playing the piano.

When it was done, Jenna **WAS** exhausted, from all the laughing. As everyone left the room and said goodnight, Dad was the last to leave. He looked at her, said goodnight and before he could shut the light, Jenna was fast asleep. Her "battery" was finally empty.

Every night after, when it was time for bed, Jenna would say her goodnights to everyone, race upstairs, floss and brush her teeth and wait for someone to come up and sing the "Little Lamb Song," and when it was done, she would fall fast asleep.

If you are having trouble falling asleep at bedtime,
maybe you could try the "Little Lamb Song" too!

I'm just a little lamb, look at me,
I'm just a little lamb, cute as can be,
I'm just a little lamb, My daddy loves me,
I'm just a little lamb, he tickles me !!

Good Night Little Lambs.

The End.

Dedications :

To my Original "Little Lambs",
Kayla, Ashley, Katelyn, and Marissa. Anything is possible.
You can ALWAYS achieve, but you must always believe!
I Love you, Always,
Dad XO

To Sandra, My Mother.
Thank you for your endless inspiring acts, your push for
betterment of self and for being the best Matriarch of
our little family, Mother and Grandmother.
YOU. ARE. MY. HERO.
If it is in writing, it must be true!
You have been a dedicated Head Start educator (Ms. Sandy)
who has read to hundreds of children during your selfless career.
Here is one more for you.
Love,
Your Son XO

To My ANAs, (Mariana, Tatiana, and Adriana):
I thank the Great Architect of the Universe for you being part of
the adventure we call life!
Family is not always just who you are related to by blood.
Lots of Love to you all. XO

About the Author

Ed Pacheco is a Dad, Husband and Entrepreneur. The idea of this story started about 20 years ago, while tucking his children into bed. His youngest daughter, recently completing elementary school prompted him to finish his work. In his spare time, Ed also does various charitable work in his community and in collaboration with his Masonic Brothers from Quittacus Lodge, in New Bedford, Massachusetts. He resides in Dartmouth, MA .

~

With deep Respect, Appreciation and Honor, the author dedicates this book to the Memory of his Father, John R. Lopes, and to his Mentor and Friend, Dr. Frederick M. Kalisz Jr. "Lucem Diffundo" Mr. Mayor.
41 38' 70.12 N , 70 55' 35.751W

Fuzzybear Press
P.O. Box 87081
South Dartmouth, MA 02748
http://fuzzybearpress.com

Paperback ISBN-13: 978-1-7332978-0-6
Hardcover ISBN-13: 978-1-7332978-1-3

Library of Congress Control Number: 2021903804

With special thanks and appreciation
Cover and interior text design by Eddie/ENC Graphic Services

CPSIA information can be obtained
at www.ICGtesting.com
Printed in the USA
LVHW072348220721
693311LV00018BA/321

9 781733 297813